VADER: VOLUME 5

Crisis strikes the galaxy. After the destruction of the DEATH STAR, the Sith Lord DARTH VADER has been deemed responsible by Emperor Palpatine. Dishonored, Vader now seeks his own agenda - the identity of the Force-strong rebel pilot responsible for the Death Star's ruin.

Enlisting the assistance of archaeologist DOCTOR APHRA, Vader has acquired a personal army composed of battle droids from a forgotten factory on the planet Geonosis. And with the help of Black Krrsantan and droids Triple-Zero and BT, Vader has captured the mysterious agent CYLO-IV who is secretly working for the Emperor.

Now with the might of an army under his hand, Vader sets out to the far reaches of space to hunt down those whom the Emperor has deemed worthy enough to replace the Dark Lord of the Sith....

KIERON GILLEN
Writer

SALVADOR LARROCA
Artist

EDGAR DELGADO
Colorist

VC's JOE CARAMAGNA
Letterer

ADI GRANOV
Cover Artist

HEATHER ANTOS
Assistant Editor

JORDAN D. WHITE
Editor

C.B. CEBULSKI & MIKE MARTS
Executive Editors

AXEL ALONSO
Editor In Chief

JOE QUESADA
Chief Creative Officer

DAN BUCKLEY
Publisher

For Lucasfilm:
Senior Editor **JENNIFER HEDDLE**
Creative Director **MICHAEL SIGLAIN**
Lucasfilm Story Group **RAYNE ROBERTS, PABLO HIDALGO, LELAND CHEE**

ABDO
Spotlight

ABDOPUBLISHING.COM

Reinforced library bound edition published in 2017 by Spotlight,
a division of ABDO, PO Box 398166, Minneapolis, Minnesota 55439.
Spotlight produces high-quality reinforced library bound editions for
schools and libraries. Published by agreement with Marvel Characters, Inc.

Printed in the United States of America, North Mankato, Minnesota.
042016
092016

THIS BOOK CONTAINS
RECYCLED MATERIALS

marvelkids.com

STAR WARS © & TM 2016 LUCASFILM LTD.

PUBLISHER'S CATALOGING IN PUBLICATION DATA

Names: Gillen, Kieron, author. | Larroca, Salvador ; Delgado, Edgar, illustrators.
Title: Vader / by Kieron Gillen ; illustrated by Salvador Larroca and Edgar Delgado.
Description: Minneapolis, MN : Spotlight, [2017] | Series: Star Wars : Darth Vader
Summary: Follow Vader straight from the ending of A New Hope into his own solo
    adventures-showing the Empire's war with the Rebel Alliance from the other
    side! When the Dark Lord needs help, to whom can he turn?
Identifiers: LCCN 2016932362 | ISBN 9781614795209 (v.1 : lib. bdg.) | ISBN
    9781614795216 (v. 2 : lib. bdg.) | ISBN 9781614795223 (v. 3 : lib. bdg.) | ISBN
    9781614795230 (v. 4 : lib. bdg.) | ISBN 9781614795247 (v.5 : lib. bdg.) | ISBN
    9781614795254 (v. 6 : lib. bdg.)
Subjects: LCSH: Vader, Darth (Fictitious character)--Juvenile fiction. | Star Wars
    fiction--Comic books, strips, etc.--Juvenile fiction. | Graphic novels--Juvenile
    fiction.
Classification: DDC 741.5--dc23
LC record available at http://lccn.loc.gov/2016932362

Spotlight

A Division of ABDO
abdopublishing.com

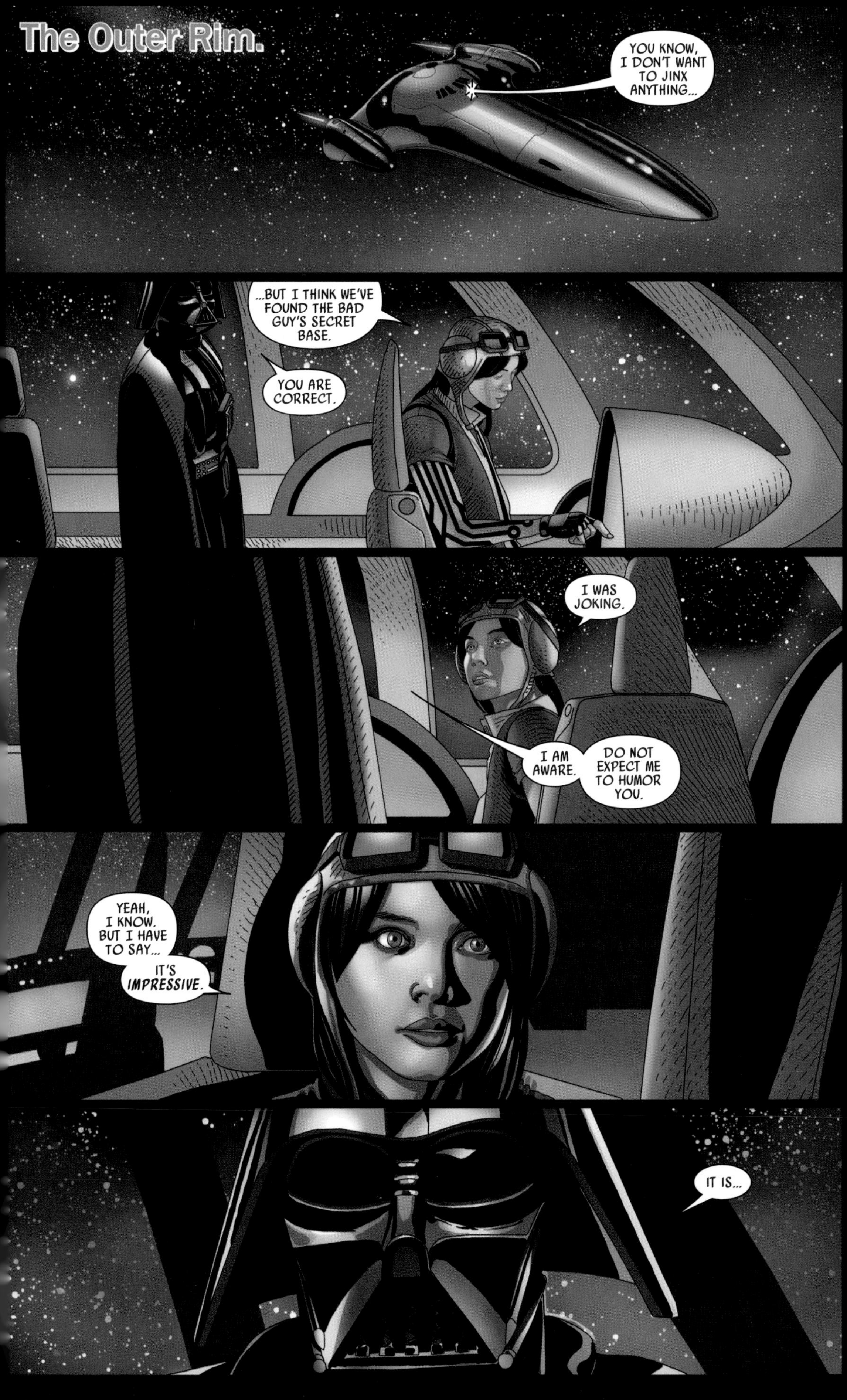

The Outer Rim.
YOU KNOW, I DON'T WANT TO JINX ANYTHING...
...BUT I THINK WE'VE FOUND THE BAD GUY'S SECRET BASE.
YOU ARE CORRECT.
I WAS JOKING.
I AM AWARE.
DO NOT EXPECT ME TO HUMOR YOU.
YEAH, I KNOW. BUT I HAVE TO SAY...
IT'S IMPRESSIVE.
IT IS...

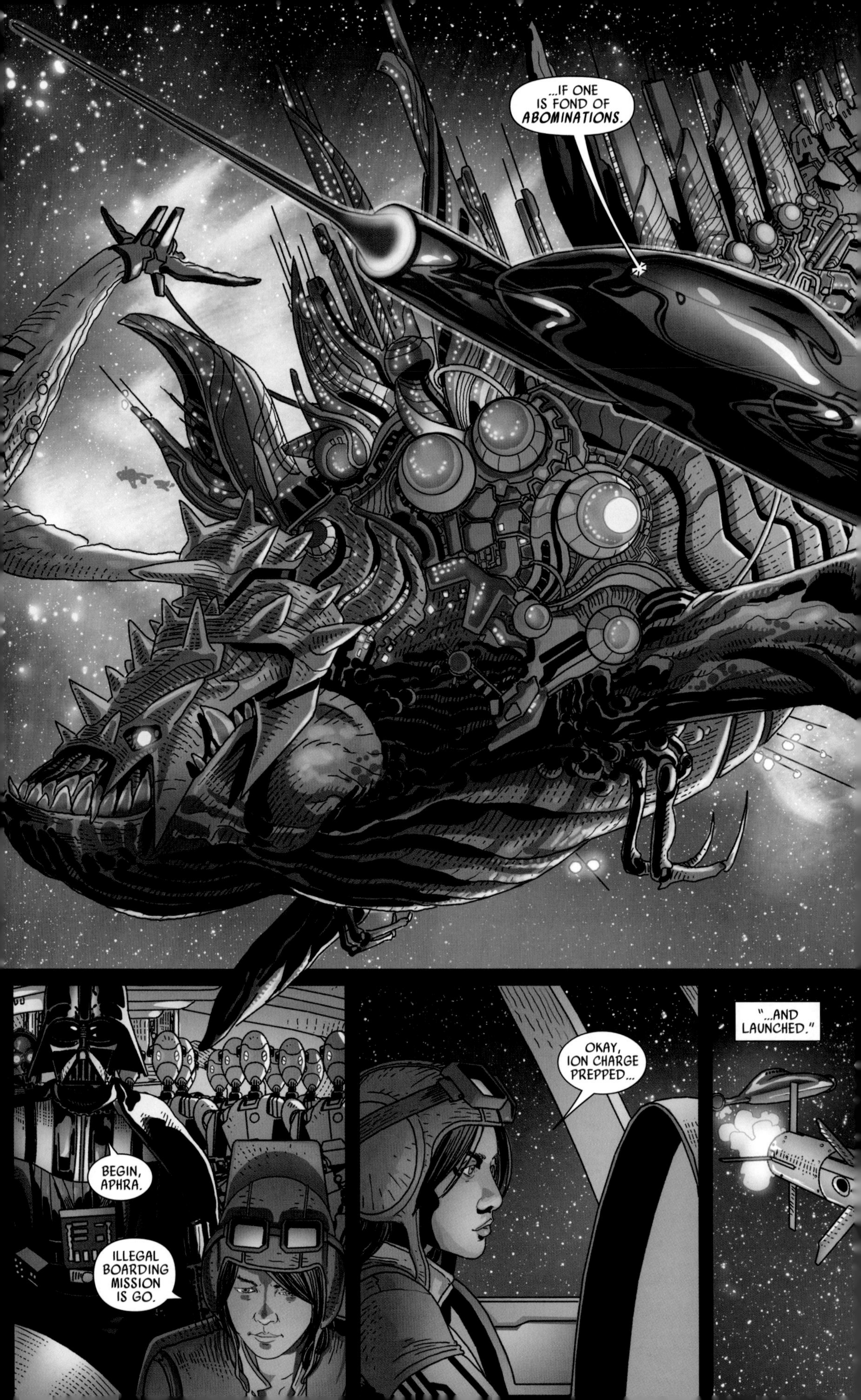
...IF ONE IS FOND OF ABOMINATIONS.
BEGIN, APHRA.
ILLEGAL BOARDING MISSION IS GO.
OKAY, ION CHARGE PREPPED...
"...AND LAUNCHED."

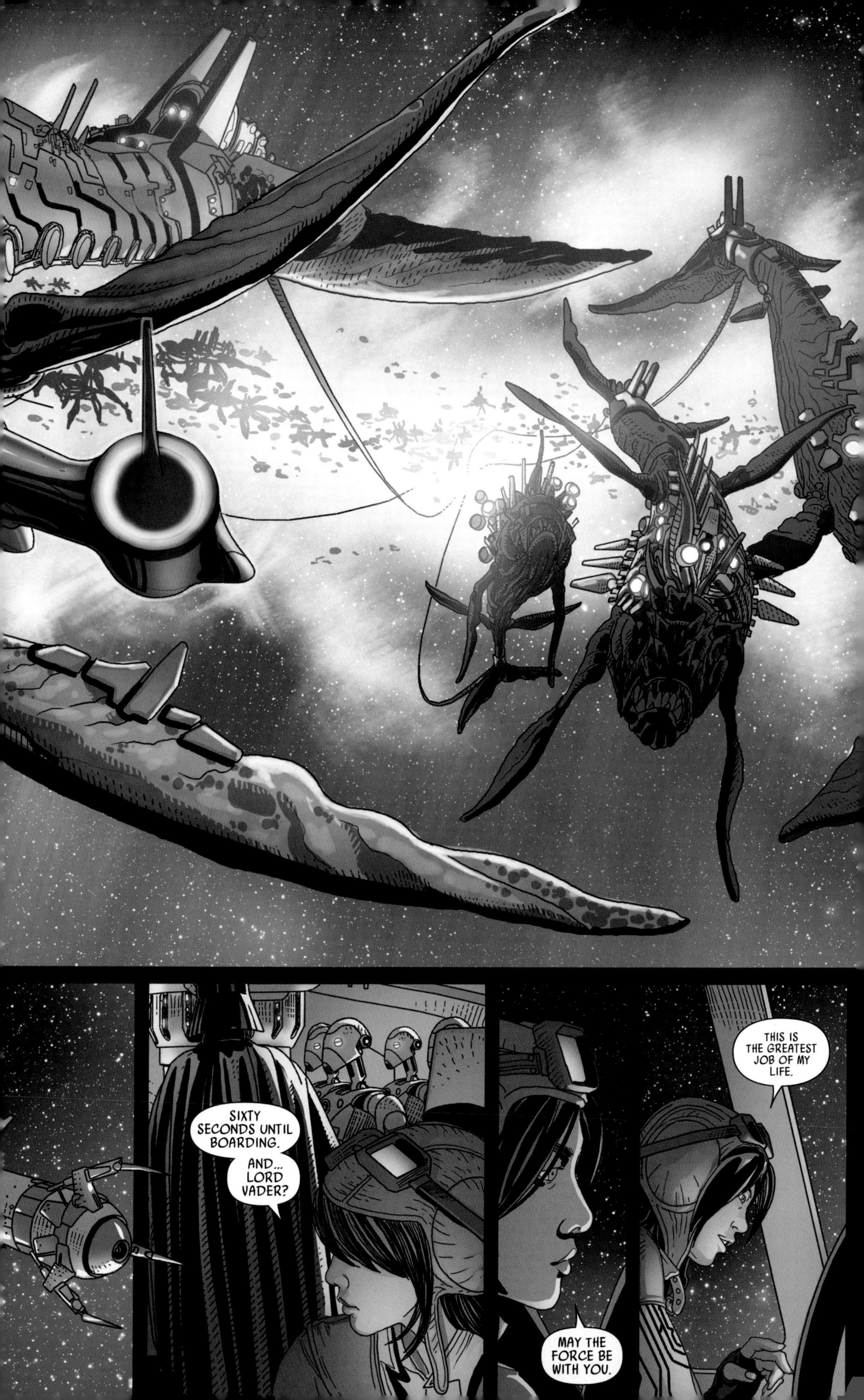

SIXTY SECONDS UNTIL BOARDING.
AND... LORD VADER?
MAY THE FORCE BE WITH YOU.
THIS IS THE GREATEST JOB OF MY LIFE.

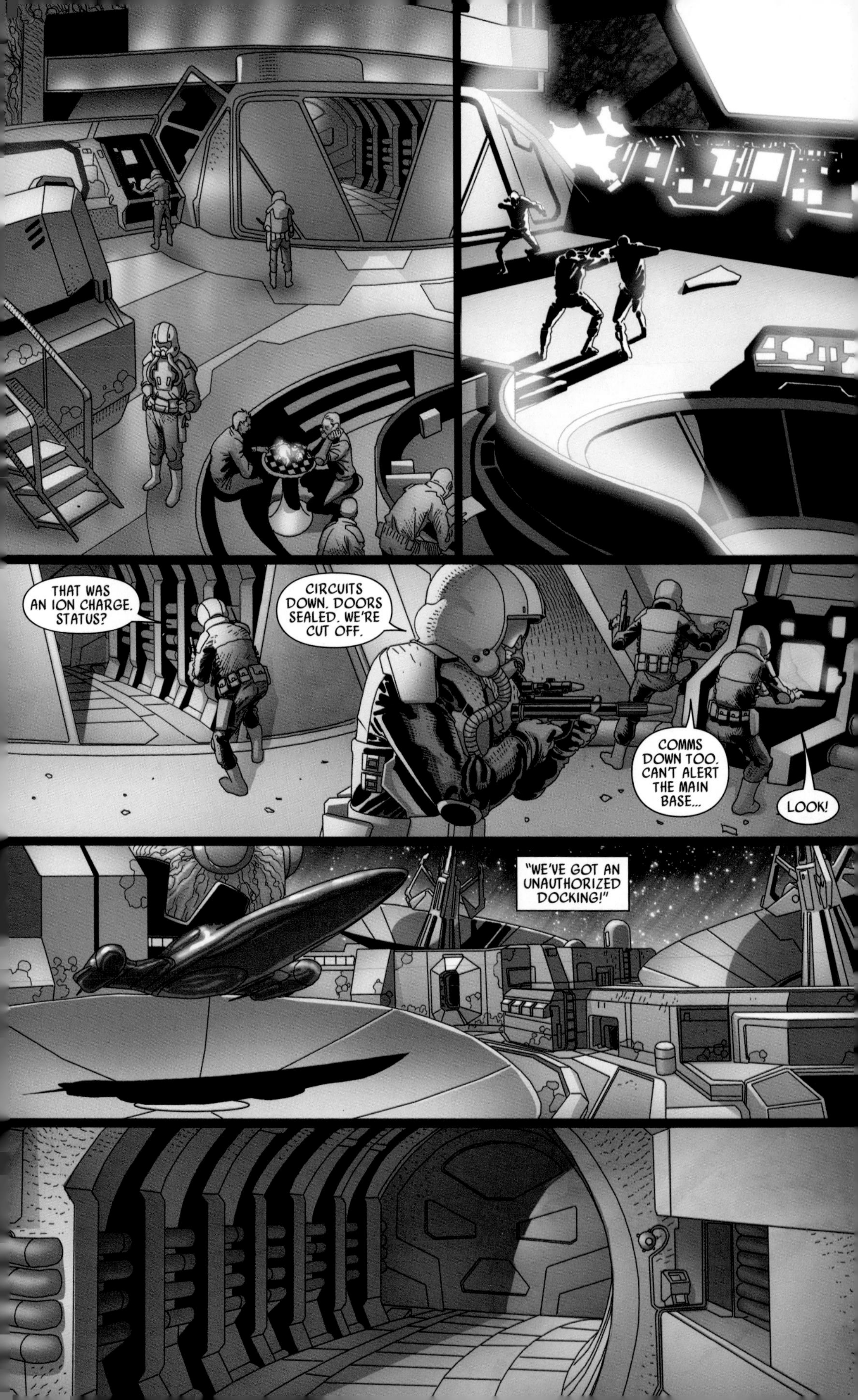
THAT WAS AN ION CHARGE. STATUS?
CIRCUITS DOWN. DOORS SEALED. WE'RE CUT OFF.
COMMS DOWN TOO. CAN'T ALERT THE MAIN BASE...
LOOK!
"WE'VE GOT AN UNAUTHORIZED DOCKING!"

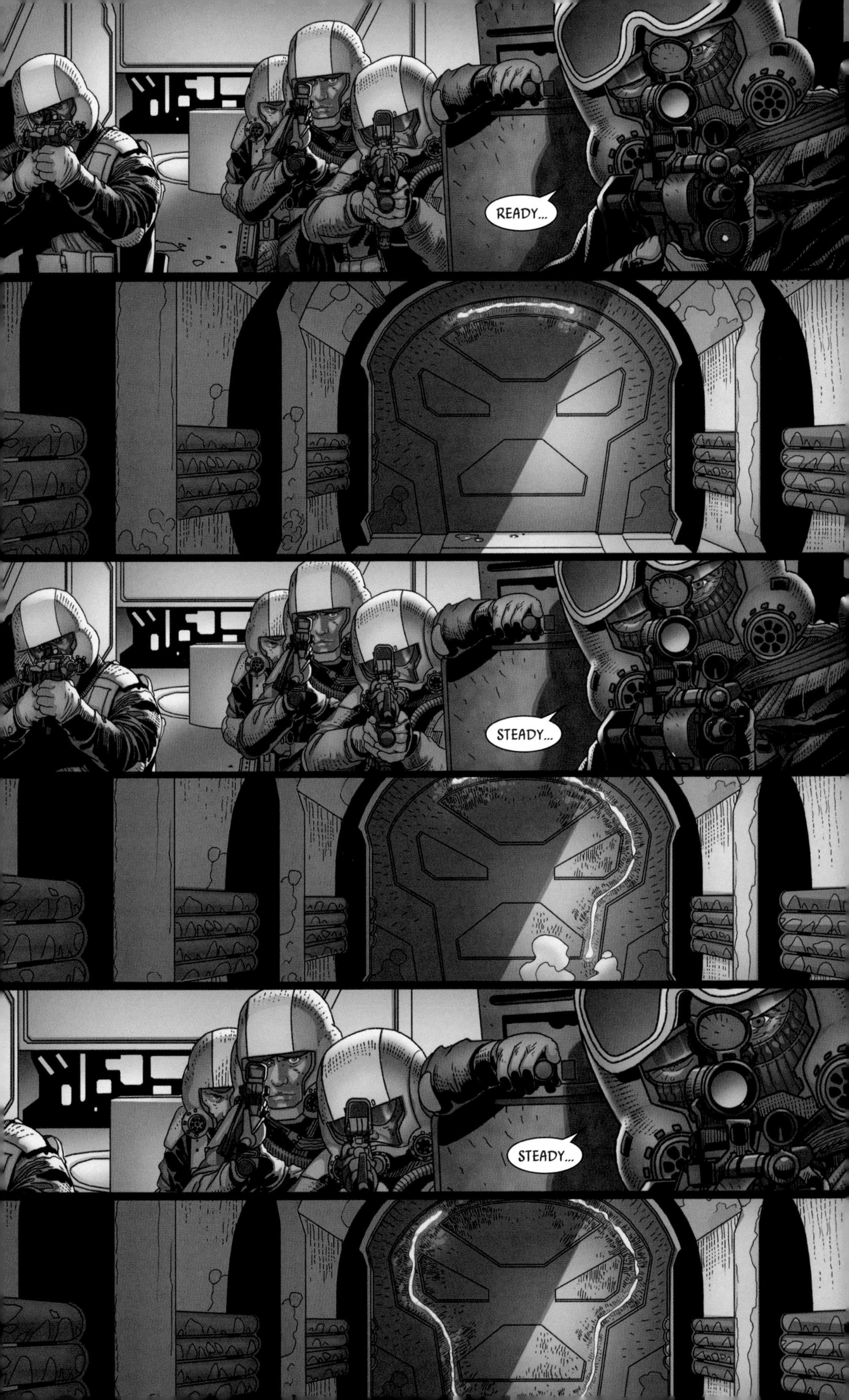
READY...
STEADY...
STEADY...

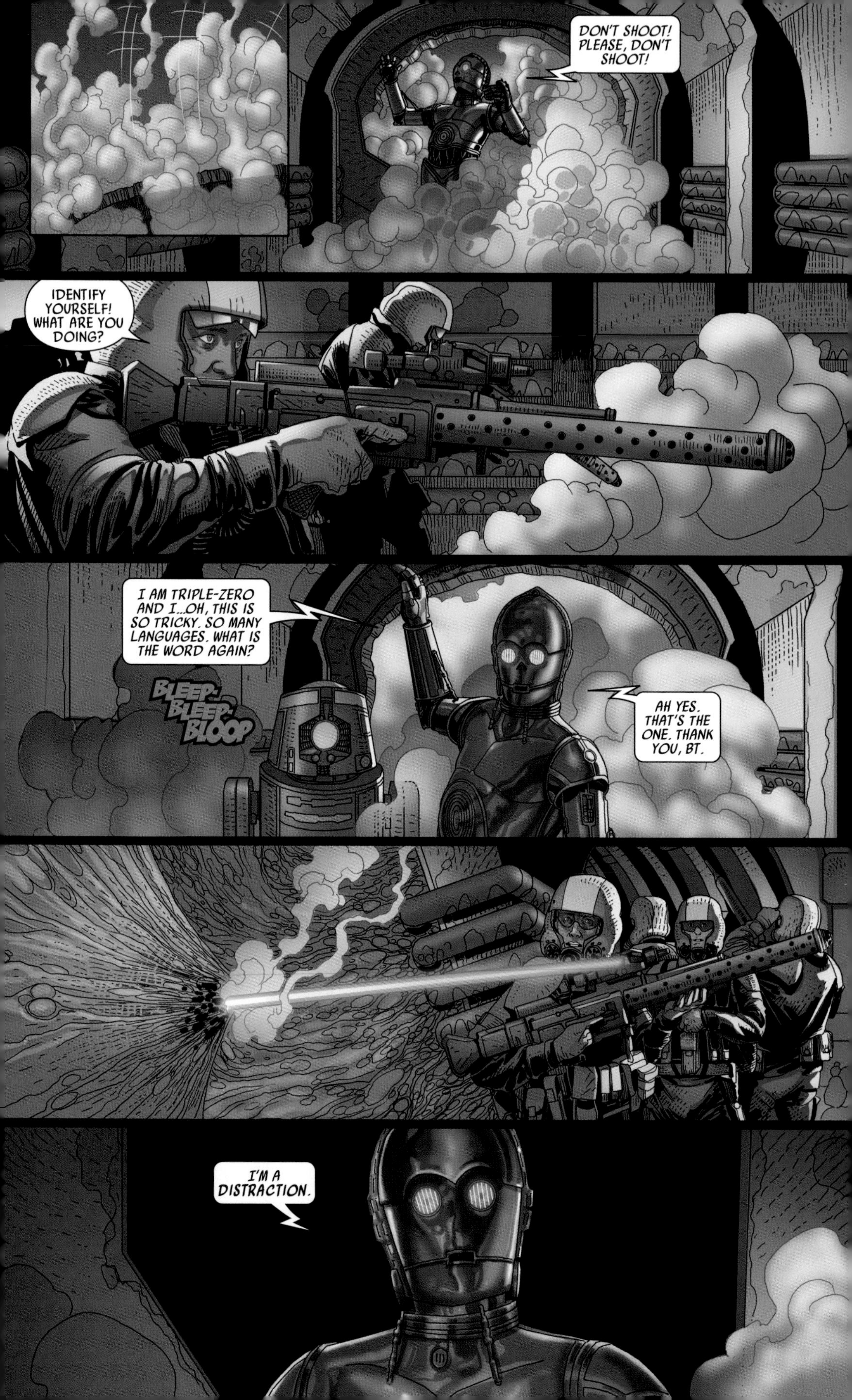
DON'T SHOOT! PLEASE, DON'T SHOOT!
IDENTIFY YOURSELF! WHAT ARE YOU DOING?
I AM TRIPLE-ZERO AND I...OH, THIS IS SO TRICKY. SO MANY LANGUAGES. WHAT IS THE WORD AGAIN?
BLEEP-BLEEP-BLOOP
AH YES. THAT'S THE ONE. THANK YOU, BT.
I'M A DISTRACTION.

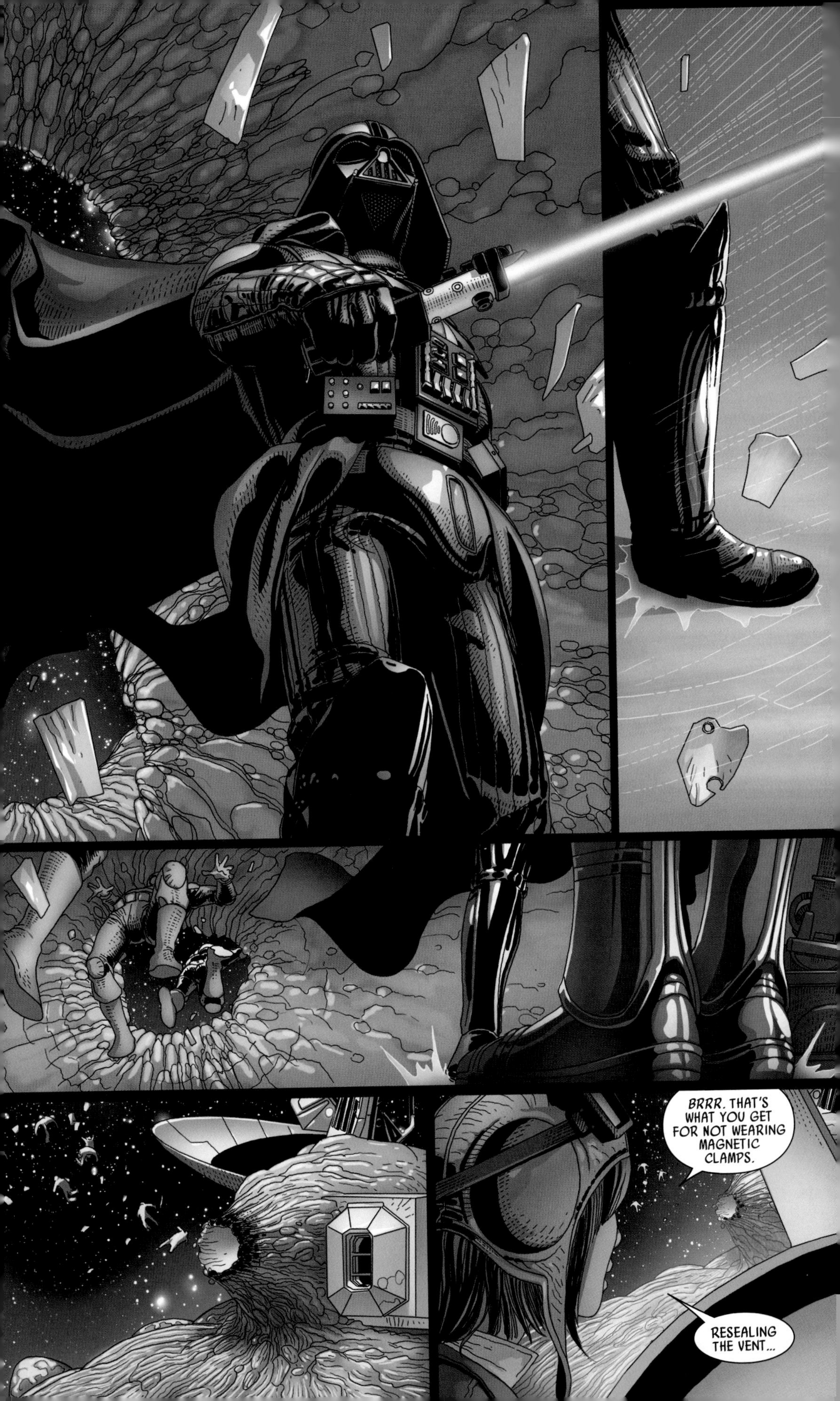
BRRR. THAT'S WHAT YOU GET FOR NOT WEARING MAGNETIC CLAMPS.
RESEALING THE VENT...

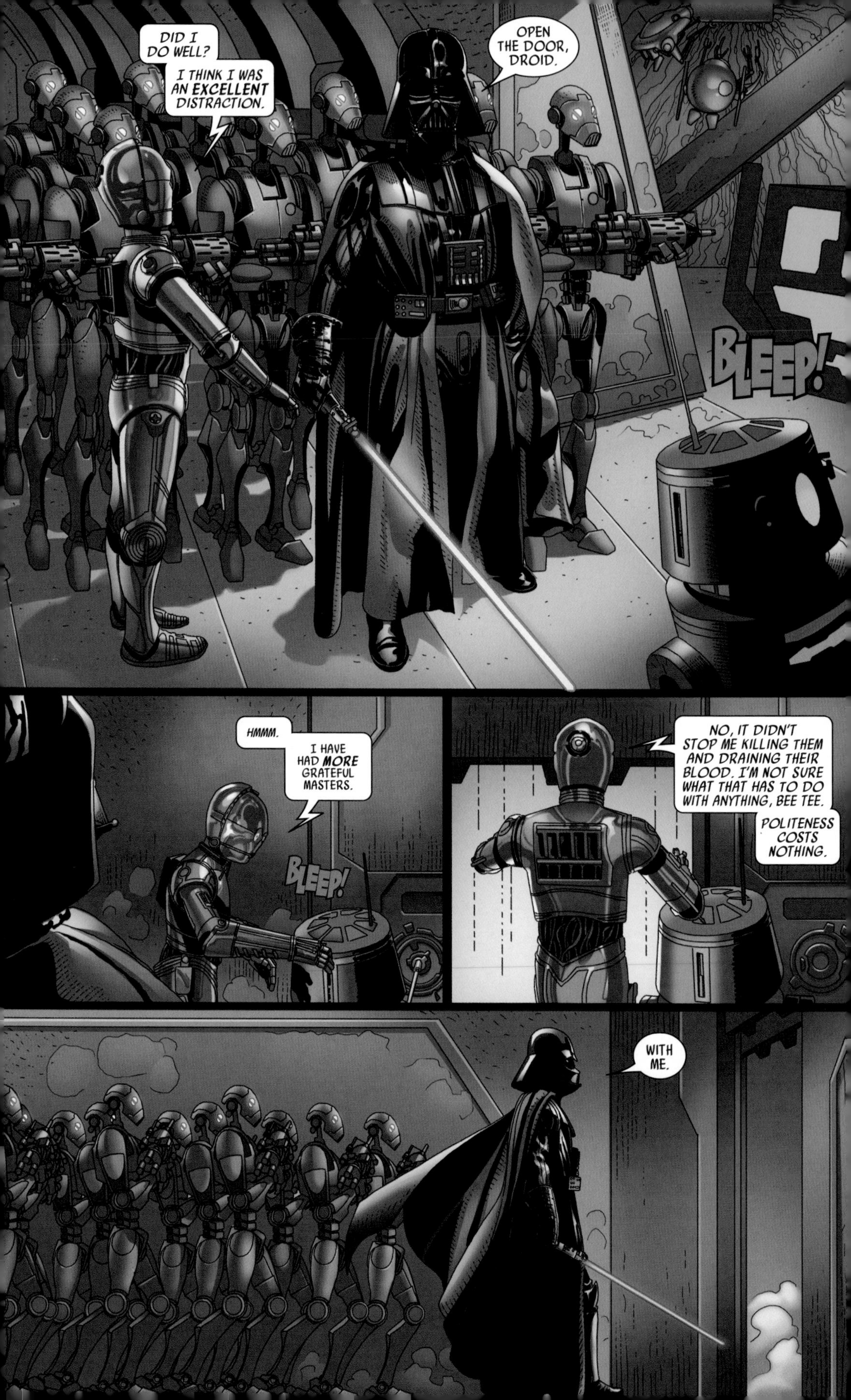
DID I DO WELL?
I THINK I WAS AN EXCELLENT DISTRACTION.
OPEN THE DOOR, DROID.
BLEEP!
HMMM.
I HAVE HAD MORE GRATEFUL MASTERS.
BLEEP!
NO, IT DIDN'T STOP ME KILLING THEM AND DRAINING THEIR BLOOD. I'M NOT SURE WHAT THAT HAS TO DO WITH ANYTHING, BEE TEE.
POLITENESS COSTS NOTHING.
WITH ME.

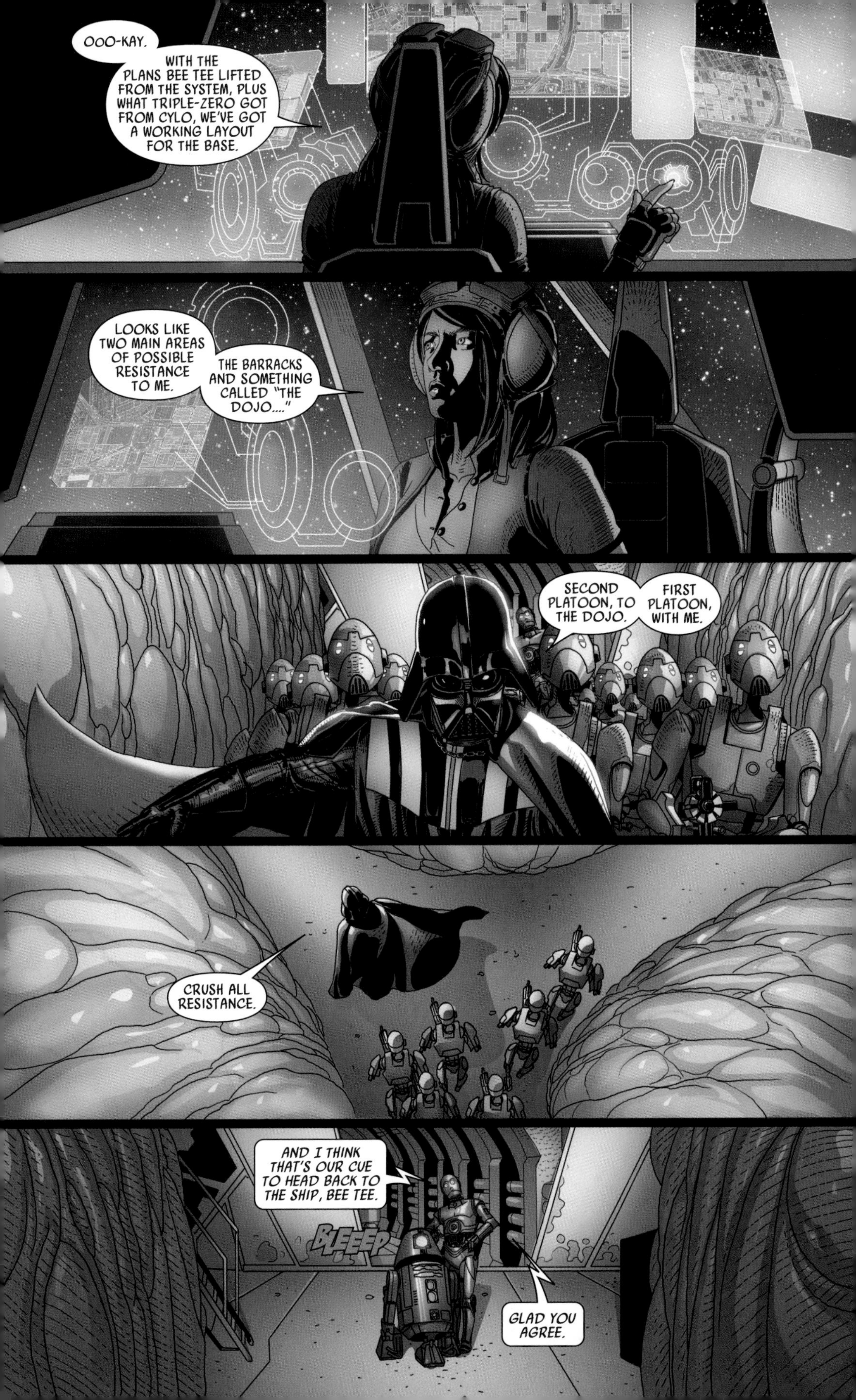
OOO-KAY.
WITH THE PLANS BEE TEE LIFTED FROM THE SYSTEM, PLUS WHAT TRIPLE-ZERO GOT FROM CYLO, WE'VE GOT A WORKING LAYOUT FOR THE BASE.
LOOKS LIKE TWO MAIN AREAS OF POSSIBLE RESISTANCE TO ME.
THE BARRACKS AND SOMETHING CALLED "THE DOJO...."
SECOND PLATOON, TO THE DOJO.
FIRST PLATOON, WITH ME.
CRUSH ALL RESISTANCE.
AND I THINK THAT'S OUR CUE TO HEAD BACK TO THE SHIP, BEE TEE.
BLEEEP
GLAD YOU AGREE.

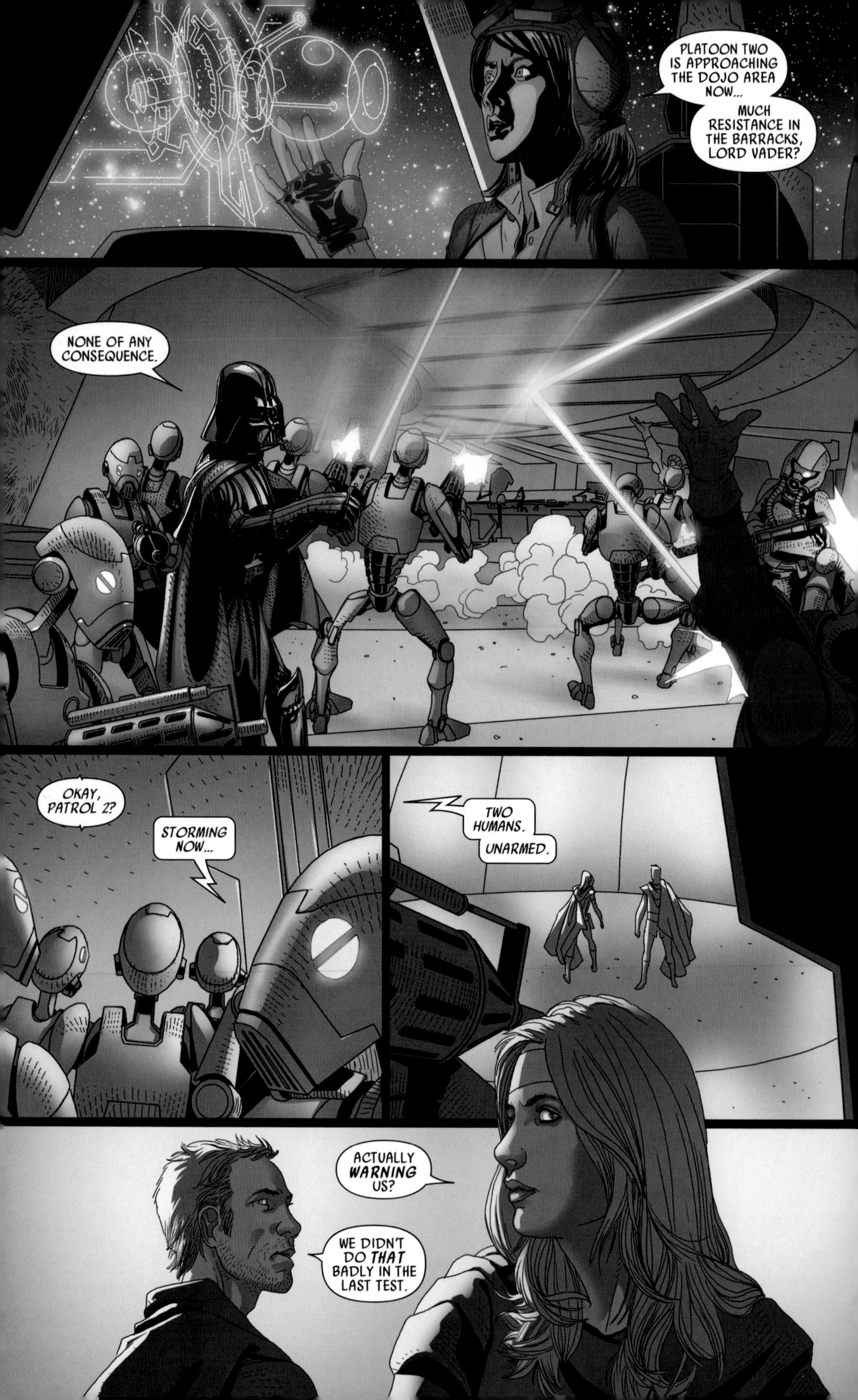
PLATOON TWO IS APPROACHING THE DOJO AREA NOW...
MUCH RESISTANCE IN THE BARRACKS, LORD VADER?
NONE OF ANY CONSEQUENCE.
OKAY, PATROL 2?
STORMING NOW...
TWO HUMANS.
UNARMED.
ACTUALLY WARNING US?
WE DIDN'T DO THAT BADLY IN THE LAST TEST.

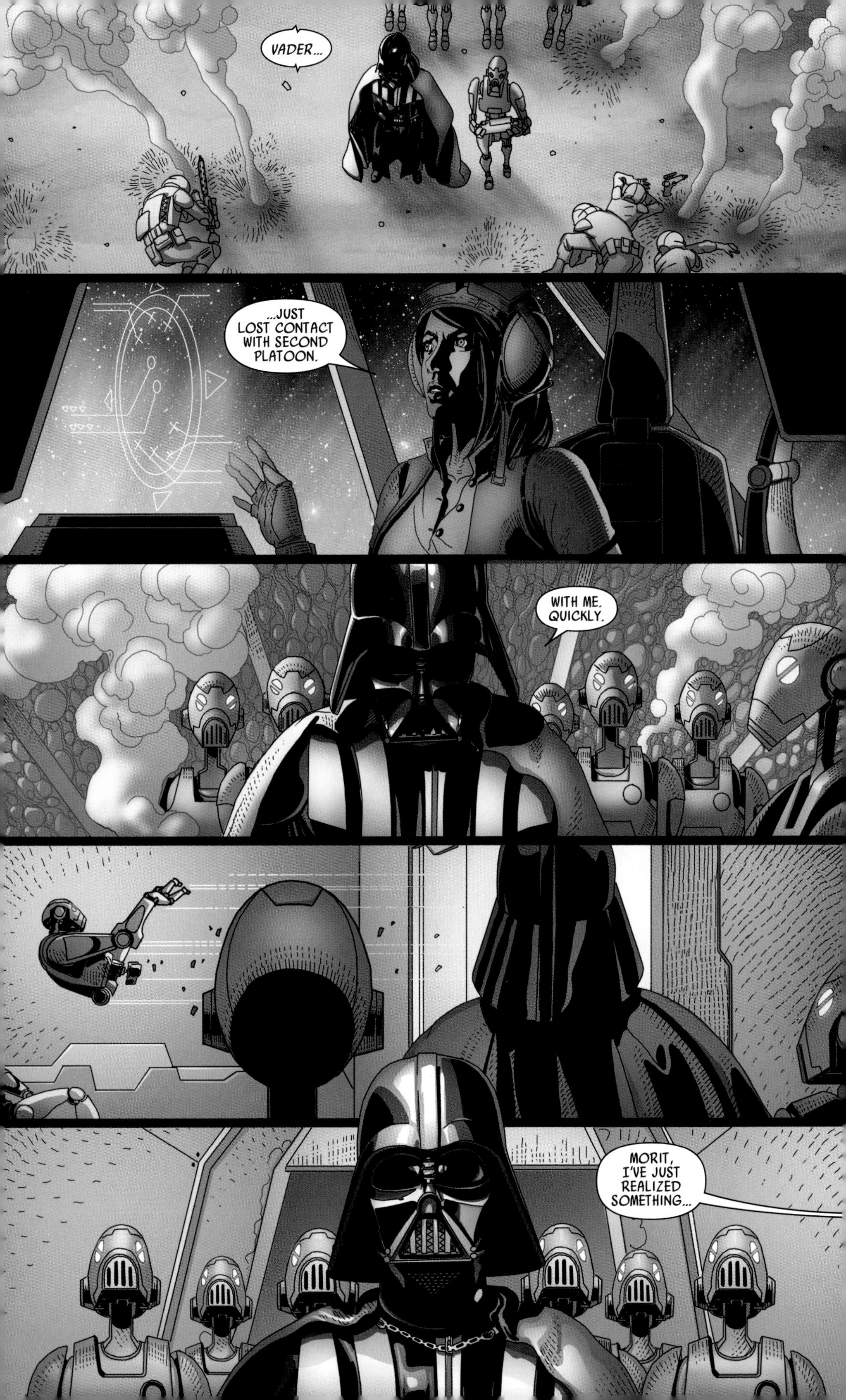
VADER...
...JUST LOST CONTACT WITH SECOND PLATOON.
WITH ME. QUICKLY.
MORIT, I'VE JUST REALIZED SOMETHING...

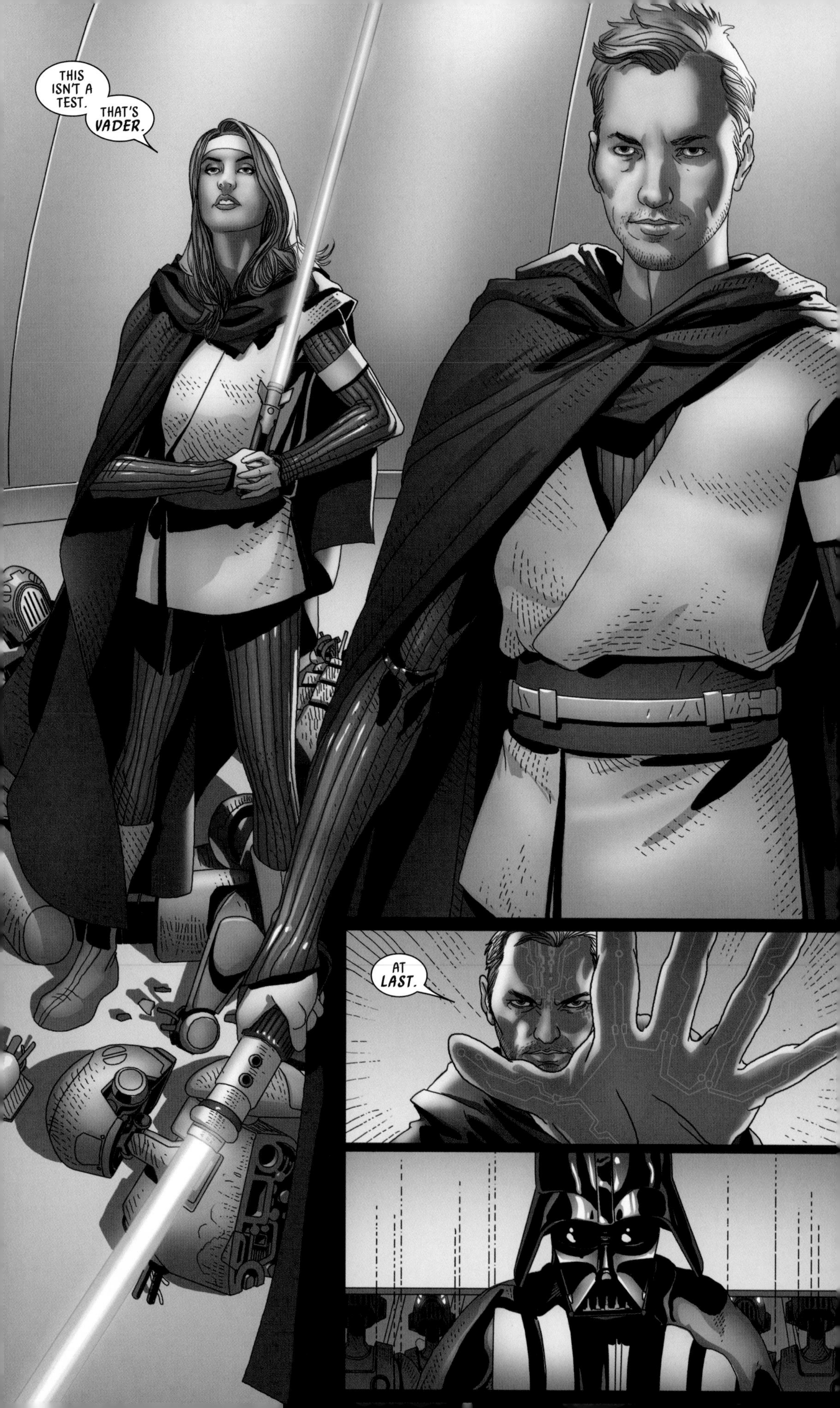
THIS ISN'T A TEST.
THAT'S VADER.
AT LAST.

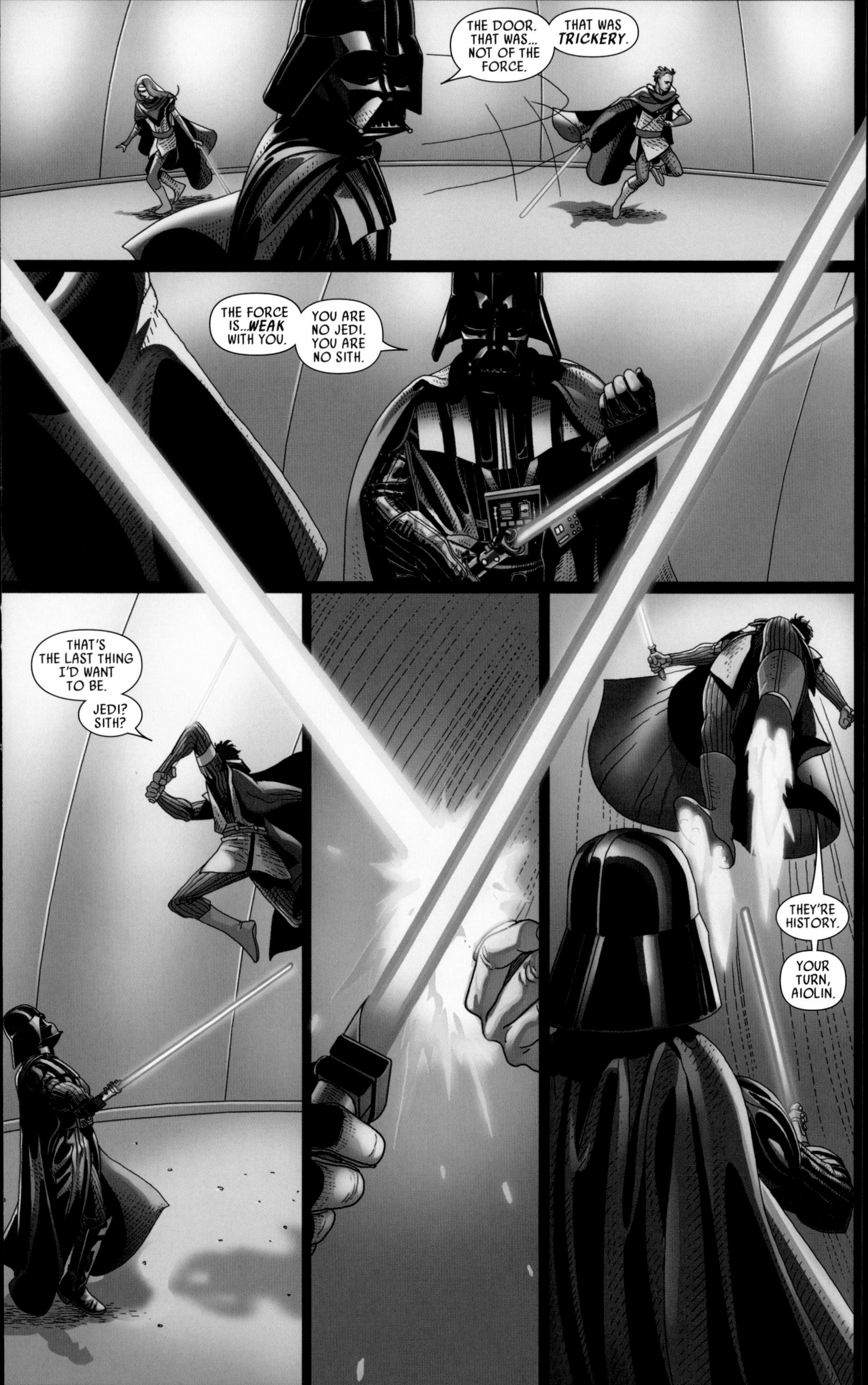
THE DOOR. THAT WAS... NOT OF THE FORCE.
THAT WAS TRICKERY.
THE FORCE IS...WEAK WITH YOU.
YOU ARE NO JEDI. YOU ARE NO SITH.
THAT'S THE LAST THING I'D WANT TO BE.
JEDI? SITH?
THEY'RE HISTORY.
YOUR TURN, AIOLIN.

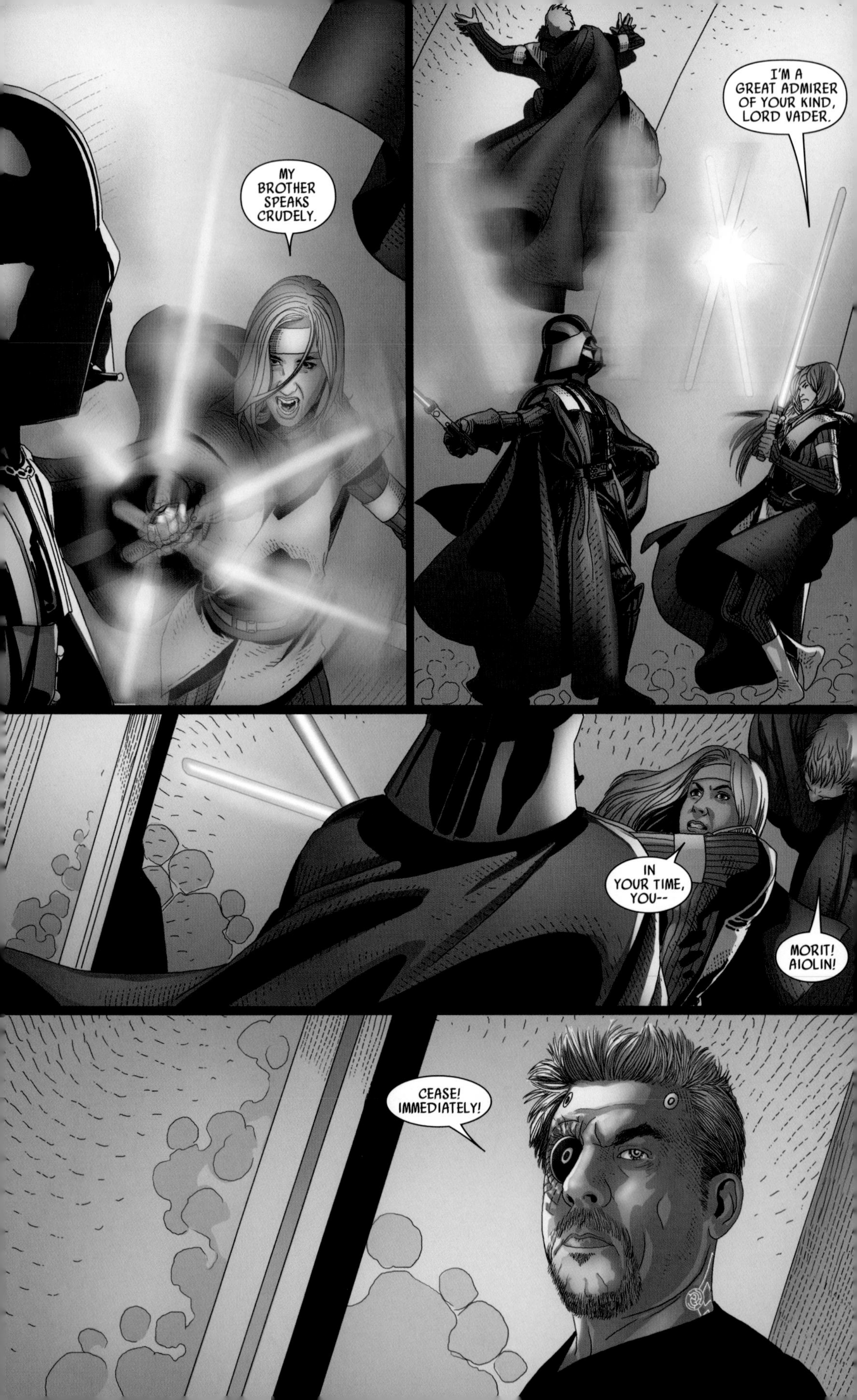
MY BROTHER SPEAKS CRUDELY.
I'M A GREAT ADMIRER OF YOUR KIND, LORD VADER.
IN YOUR TIME, YOU--
MORIT! AIOLIN!
CEASE! IMMEDIATELY!

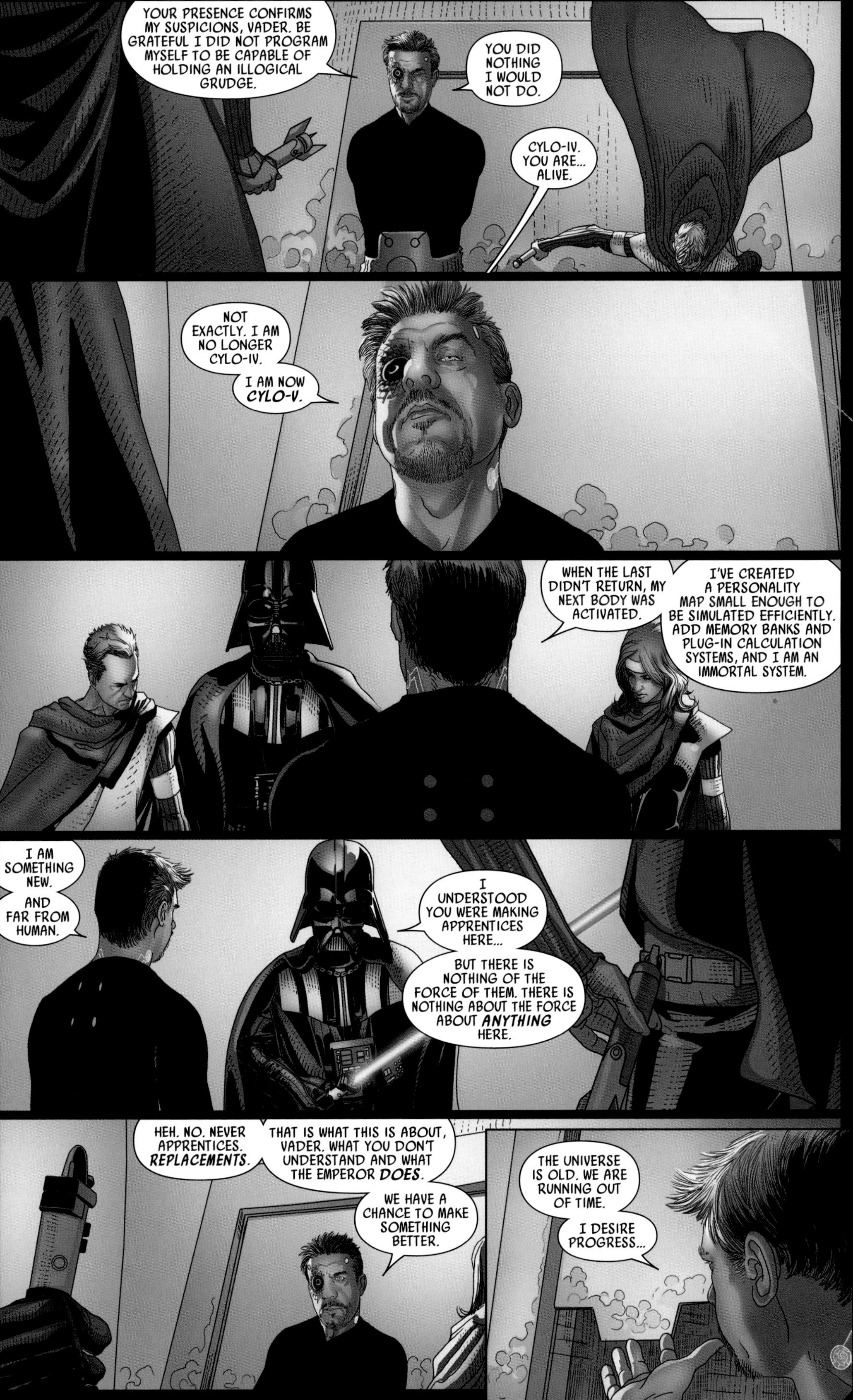
YOUR PRESENCE CONFIRMS MY SUSPICIONS, VADER. BE GRATEFUL I DID NOT PROGRAM MYSELF TO BE CAPABLE OF HOLDING AN ILLOGICAL GRUDGE.
YOU DID NOTHING I WOULD NOT DO.
CYLO-IV. YOU ARE... ALIVE.
NOT EXACTLY. I AM NO LONGER CYLO-IV.
I AM NOW *CYLO-V.*
WHEN THE LAST DIDN'T RETURN, MY NEXT BODY WAS ACTIVATED.
I'VE CREATED A PERSONALITY MAP SMALL ENOUGH TO BE SIMULATED EFFICIENTLY. ADD MEMORY BANKS AND PLUG-IN CALCULATION SYSTEMS, AND I AM AN IMMORTAL SYSTEM.
I AM SOMETHING NEW.
AND FAR FROM HUMAN.
I UNDERSTOOD YOU WERE MAKING APPRENTICES HERE...
BUT THERE IS NOTHING OF THE FORCE OF THEM. THERE IS NOTHING ABOUT THE FORCE ABOUT *ANYTHING* HERE.
HEH. NO. NEVER APPRENTICES. *REPLACEMENTS.*
THAT IS WHAT THIS IS ABOUT, VADER. WHAT YOU DON'T UNDERSTAND AND WHAT THE EMPEROR *DOES.*
WE HAVE A CHANCE TO MAKE SOMETHING BETTER.
THE UNIVERSE IS OLD. WE ARE RUNNING OUT OF TIME.
I DESIRE PROGRESS...

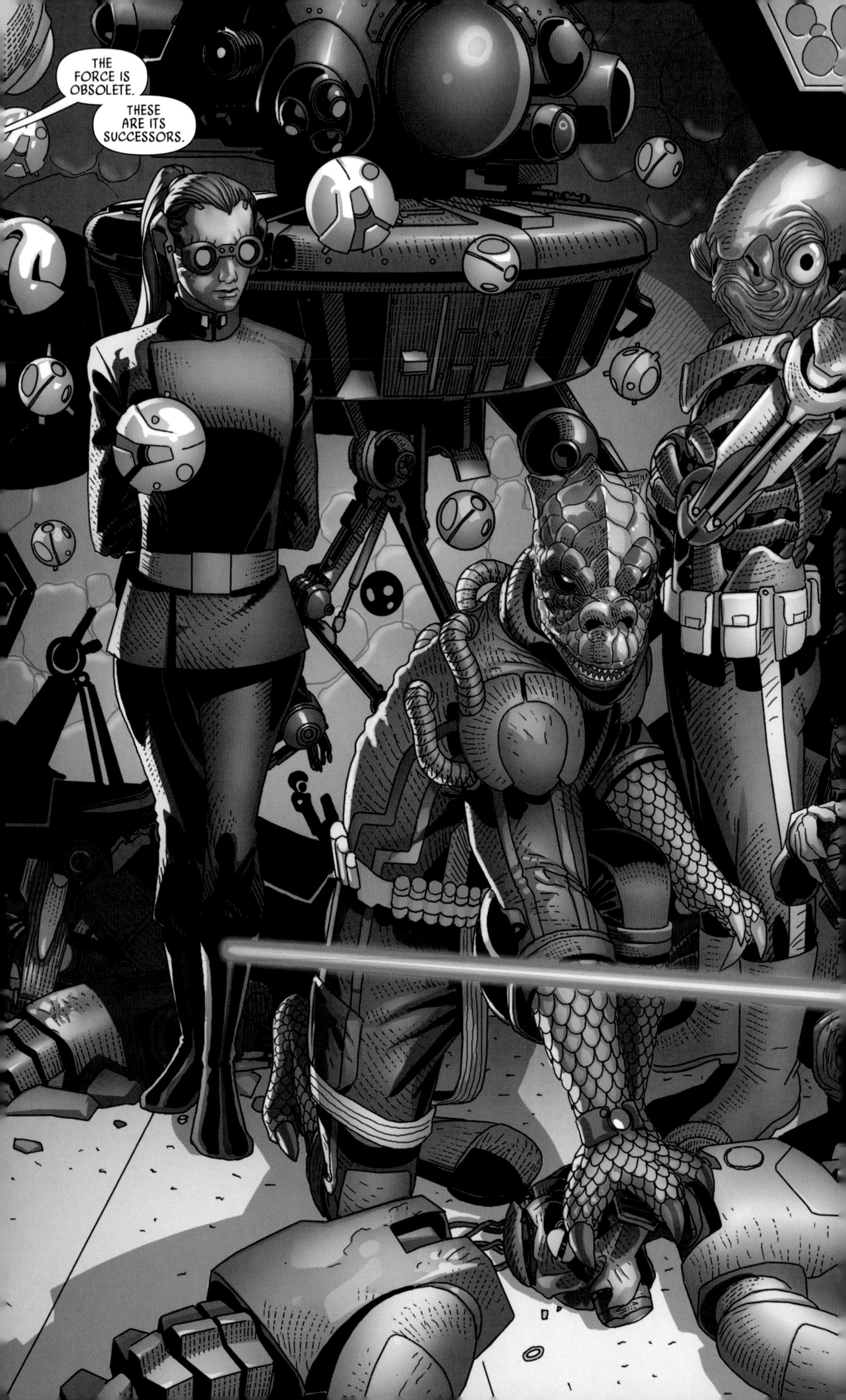
THE FORCE IS OBSOLETE.
THESE ARE ITS SUCCESSORS.

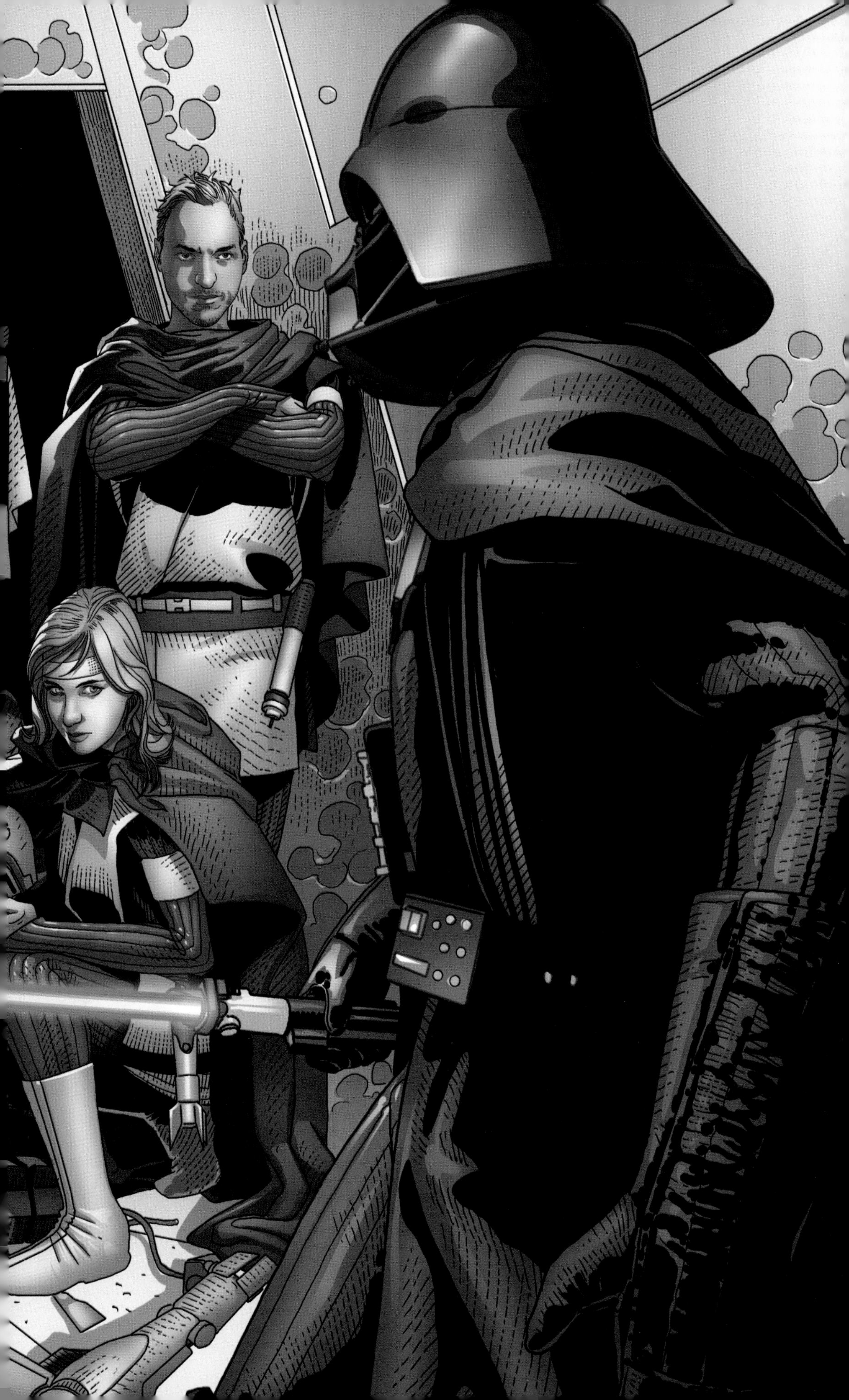

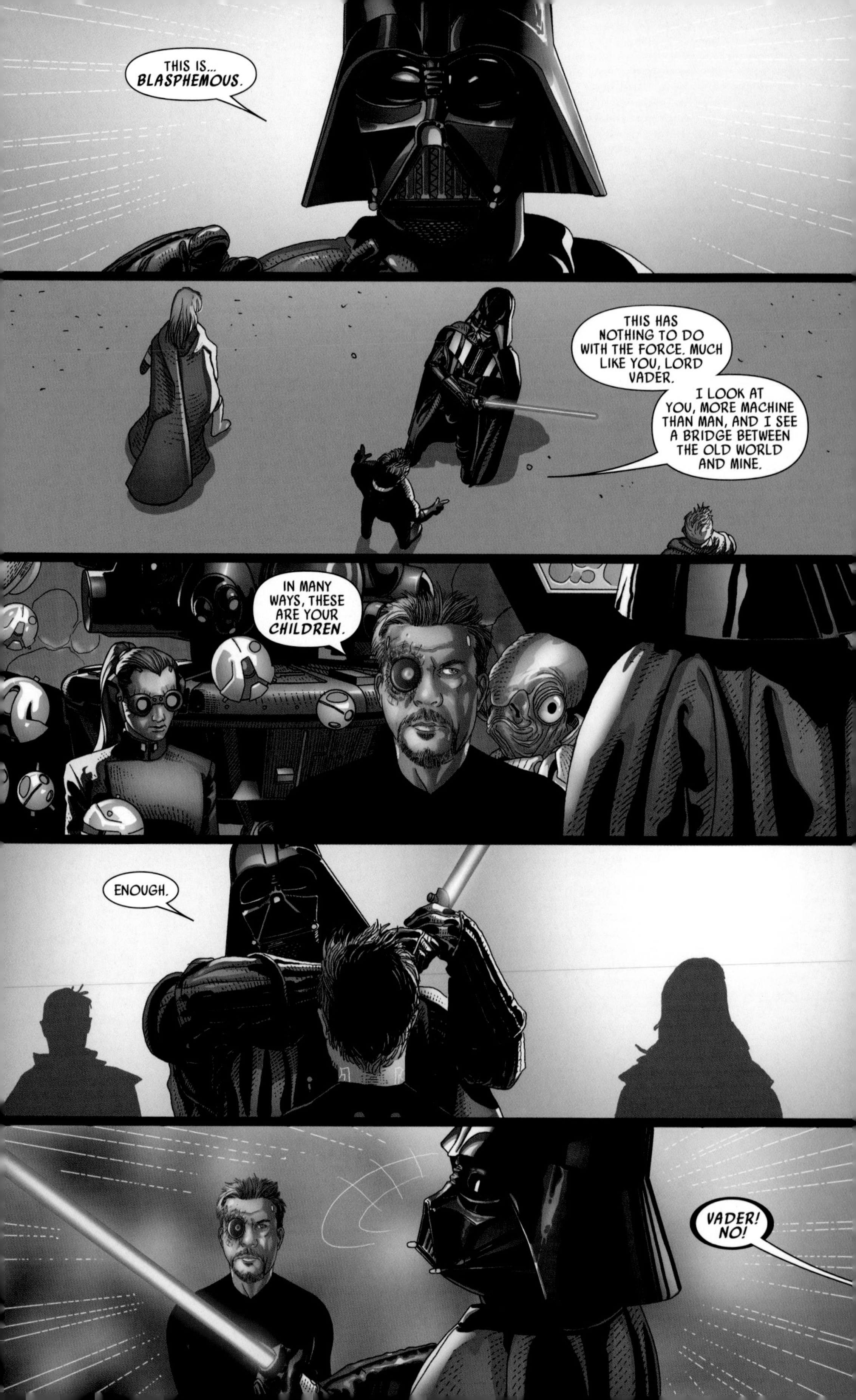
THIS IS... BLASPHEMOUS.
THIS HAS NOTHING TO DO WITH THE FORCE. MUCH LIKE YOU, LORD VADER.
I LOOK AT YOU, MORE MACHINE THAN MAN, AND I SEE A BRIDGE BETWEEN THE OLD WORLD AND MINE.
IN MANY WAYS, THESE ARE YOUR CHILDREN.
ENOUGH.
VADER! NO!

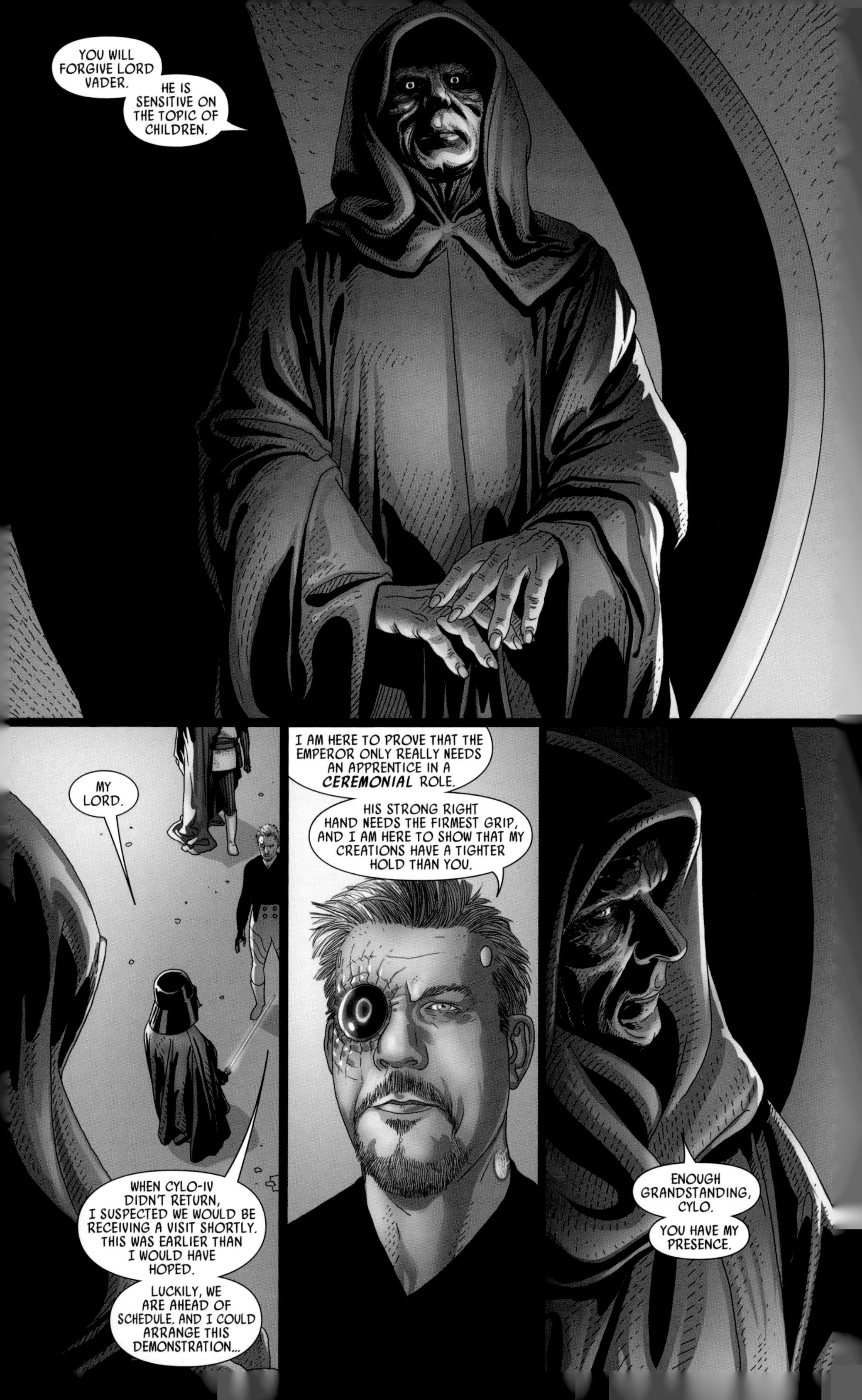
YOU WILL FORGIVE LORD VADER.
HE IS SENSITIVE ON THE TOPIC OF CHILDREN.
MY LORD.
WHEN CYLO-IV DIDN'T RETURN, I SUSPECTED WE WOULD BE RECEIVING A VISIT SHORTLY. THIS WAS EARLIER THAN I WOULD HAVE HOPED.
LUCKILY, WE ARE AHEAD OF SCHEDULE, AND I COULD ARRANGE THIS DEMONSTRATION...
I AM HERE TO PROVE THAT THE EMPEROR ONLY REALLY NEEDS AN APPRENTICE IN A CEREMONIAL ROLE.
HIS STRONG RIGHT HAND NEEDS THE FIRMEST GRIP, AND I AM HERE TO SHOW THAT MY CREATIONS HAVE A TIGHTER HOLD THAN YOU.
ENOUGH GRANDSTANDING, CYLO.
YOU HAVE MY PRESENCE.

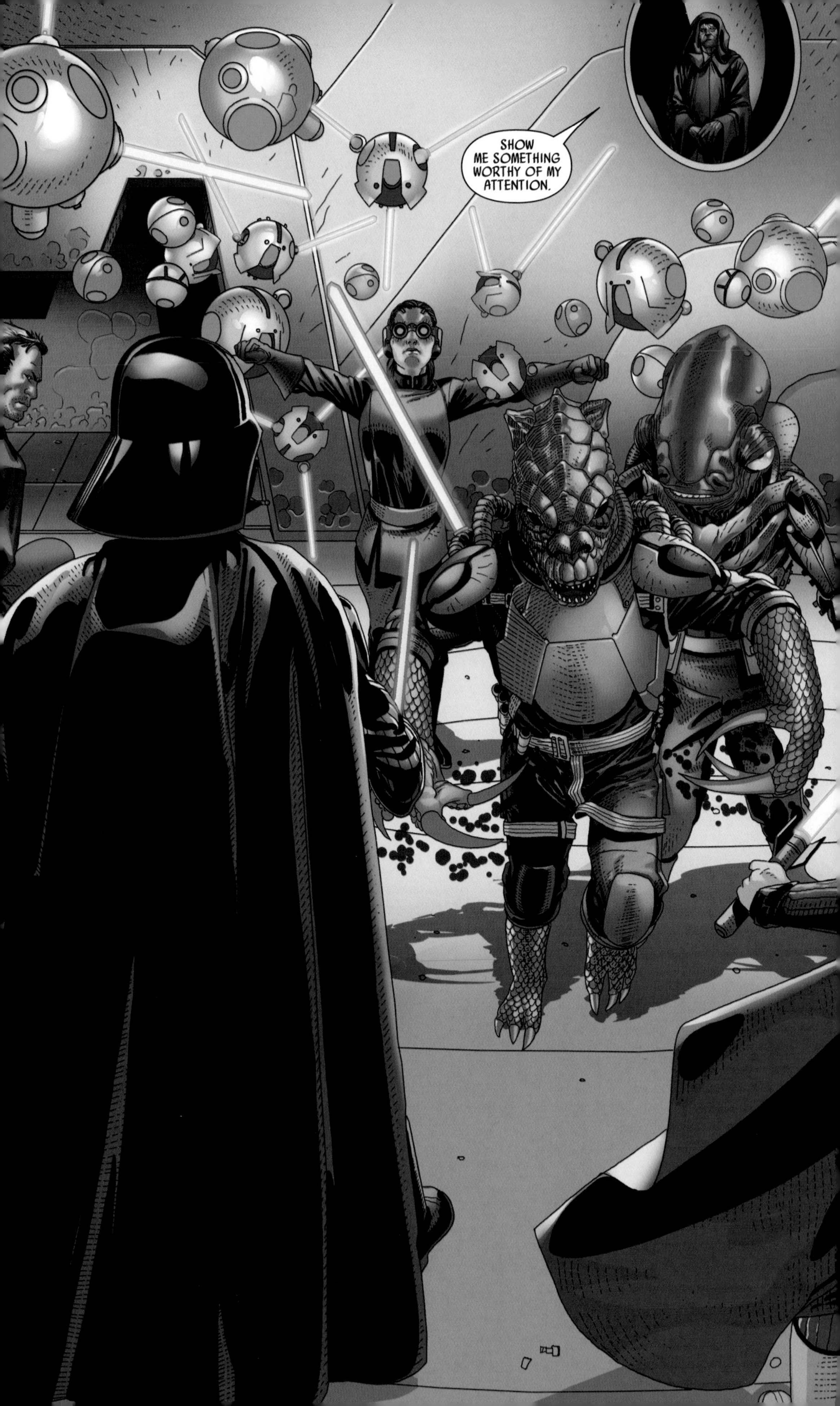
SHOW ME SOMETHING WORTHY OF MY ATTENTION.

STAR WARS®

DARTH VADER

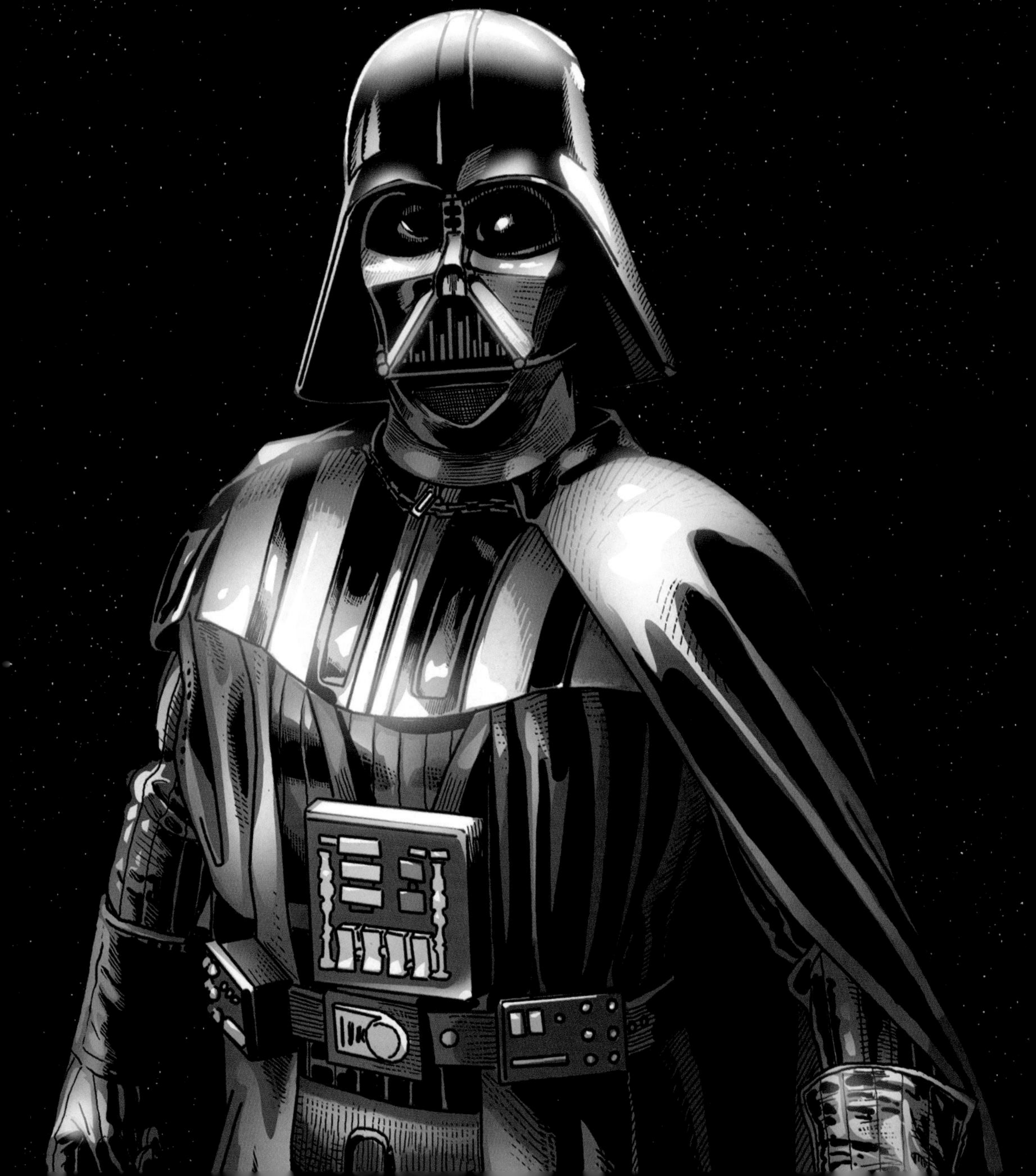

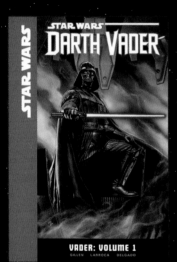
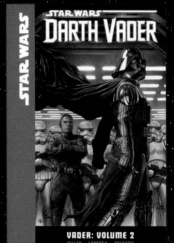
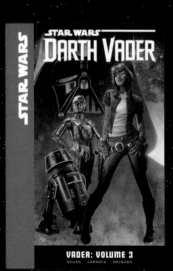
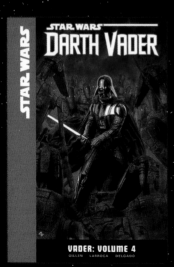
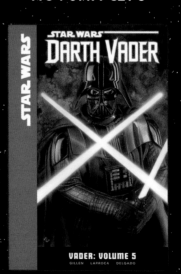